Based on the TV series Nickelodeon Avatar: The Last Airbender™ as seen on Nickelodeon®

SIMON SPOTLIGHT
An imprint of Simon & Schuster Children's Publishing Division
1230 Avenue of the Americas, New York, New York 10020
© 2007 Viacom International Inc. All rights reserved. NICKELODEON, Nickelodeon Avatar: The Last Airbender, and all related titles, logos, and characters are trademarks of Viacom International Inc.
All rights reserved, including the right of reproduction in whole or in part in any form. SIMON SPOTLIGHT and colophon are registered trademarks of Simon & Schuster, Inc.
Manufactured in the United States of America
3 4 5 6 7 8 9 10
ISBN-13: 978-1-4169-3797-5
ISBN-10: 1-4169-3797-8
Library of Congress Catalog Card Number 2007925258

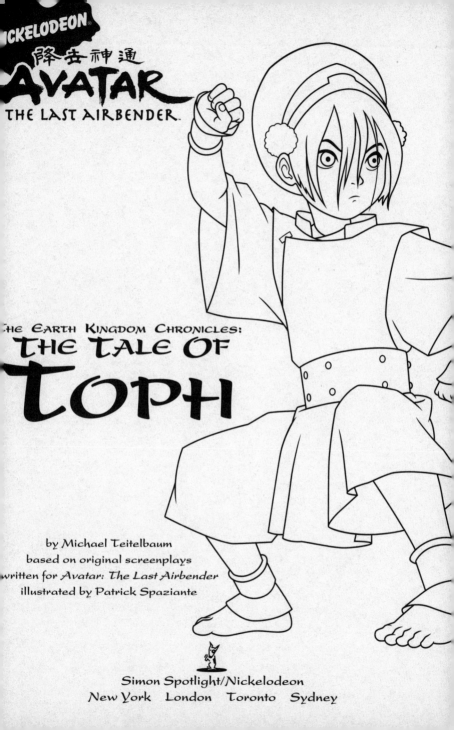

NICKELODEON

降去神通

AVATAR

THE LAST AIRBENDER.

THE EARTH KINGDOM CHRONICLES:
THE TALE OF
TOPH

by Michael Teitelbaum
based on original screenplays
written for *Avatar: The Last Airbender*
illustrated by Patrick Spaziante

Simon Spotlight/Nickelodeon
New York   London   Toronto   Sydney

Chapter 1

My name is Toph Beifong. I'm an Earthbender. 5
A pretty good one, too. But what really stinks is
that I have to hide that part of who I am.

See, my parents are very rich and power—
ful. I come from one of the most important
families in the Earth Kingdom, the Beifongs.
Just saying my last name has always opened
doors. People rush to help me just because my
family is wealthy, and I really can't stand that.

I live on a huge estate in a giant mansion,
with servants attending to my every whim. I hate
that, too. I don't want to be treated as royalty
or anyone special. And I most definitely do not

want to be treated as if I have a handicap.

Oh, yeah, I guess I should mention that I'm blind. But before you start feeling sorry for me or start thinking I'm helpless, let me explain something. I see with my feet. I know it sounds weird, but believe me, it's true. More accurately, I see using Earthbending. I feel the vibrations in the earth and they help me figure out where everything is. I can sense the slightest movement—in other people, in tree branches swaying in the wind, even in the tiniest ants crawling on the ground.

I've never felt sorry for myself for one second, but my parents don't understand me. They always treat me like I'm helpless. They think I'm just a beginning-level Earthbending student, and they take comfort in that. If I ever showed them what I'm really capable of, they'd ground me for the next twenty years!

Sometimes I get so frustrated from hiding who I really am, not being able to use my Earthbending skills to their full capacity around my mom and dad, I feel like screaming! So, that's why I've adopted a kind of secret identity.

I sneak out of my house at night, when my

parents are asleep, and I compete in Earthbending tournaments. If my folks ever found out about it, I'd be grounded for the rest of my life! At the competitions I'm known as "the Blind Bandit." It's kind of silly, I know. But I didn't even make up the name. This guy named Xin Fu, who runs the tournaments, started calling me that.

Competing lets me cut loose with my Earthbending abilities—a chance I never get as Toph Beifong, poor, weak, blind girl, obedient daughter of the oh-so-important Beifong family. But as the Blind Bandit, I fight—and win, by the way. In fact, I'M the reigning champion!

Tonight is Earth Rumble Six. The arena is packed. After a particularly boring day "studying" with my Earthbending teacher, Master Yu, "learning" how to move tiny pebbles, I'm ready to kick some Earthbending butt.

As the champ, I get to sit back and watch a bunch of chumps compete until they narrow the challengers down. My opponent tonight is this big, muscle-bound guy who calls himself "the Boulder." I think he got the name because he moves as slowly and stomps as heavily as one, not because he Earthbends them well.

Okay, here it goes. . . . I love it when the crowd cheers like this!

"The Boulder feels conflicted about fighting a young, blind girl!" he said aloud.

What a fool! He's going down—hard!

"Whenever you're ready, 'Pebble'!" The crowd loves this stuff. And I have to admit I get a kick out of stirring them up.

Right now I'm laughing loudly. You know, to make the Boulder even madder than he already is. The angrier an opponent, the less subtle his attack, the easier it is for me to follow his moves and stop him.

"It's on!" the Boulder cried.

Finally! Okay, Toph, focus on his movements. Block out the sound of the crowd, just feel the ground under your feet. There he is— he's charging forward—but not for long!

The Boulder went down quickly. He took a big clumsy step toward me, then lifted his other foot. Before it could hit the ground, I flexed my ankle, driving my heel into the earth, sending a narrow shockwave racing toward him. So as his foot came down, a ripple of rock from my shockwave shoved his foot to the side, causing him to land in a painful split. He moaned and groaned as he scrambled back to his feet.

Ha! Take that! Maybe one of these days they'll bring me some serious competition. In fact, maybe I'll just finish him off right now—for kicks. BAM!

I extended my arms, Earthbending three jagged poles of rock, which burst up from the ground, slammed into the Boulder, and sent him flying into the far wall. Match over.

Yawn! This is so boring—Whoa, did I just hear that right? Xin Fu's offering a sack of gold to anyone who can beat me. Finally, some real competition. What, no takers? Wait a minute, who's this little guy? He feels tiny . . . small enough to crush with my bare hands—without even using Earthbending! What'd he just say to me? He doesn't want to fight, he just wants to talk to me? I'm not here for conversation, kid. I'm here to defend my title, so bring it on!

Okay, he's in the air . . . but why hasn't he landed? Where'd he go? Is he still in the air? How can that be? I can't see him if I can't feel his movements on the ground. There he is. But he landed so softly, as if he was floating. How did he do that?

"Somebody's a little light on his feet!" I shouted. "What's your fighting name? 'The Fancy Dancer'?"

He's not getting away this time. I'll knock him right off those fancy feet.

He's gone, again! It's like he just vanished. Can this kid fly? That's impossible, but all I know is that he's not standing on the ground. Ah, there you are. An even softer landing this time. I am not amused.

Okay, no more funny business. You want to play, here's a ball, kid. Actually, here's a big fat boulder! Wait a minute, why can't I hear the boulder rolling toward him? What's happening?

BAM! I can't believe it! He just turned my boulder against me and it pushed me out of the ring! The rock never landed, and the Fancy Dancer never touched down. That must be why I couldn't pick up the rock's movement fast enough. And that's how this scrawny little kid beat me! I am so out of here!

"Wait!"

Now what? Oh, now he wants to chat!

"Please, listen!"

This kid just doesn't know when to quit!

"I need an Earthbending teacher, and I think it's supposed to be you!"

And this is my problem because . . . ?

"Whoever you are, just leave me alone!" Then I Earthbended a doorway through the wall, kept on walking, and slammed the opening shut behind me.

I don't know who this kid is or what he's talking about, but I really don't care. I'm no one's teacher, especially not some weird, flying dancer who just stole my championship title!

The very next day I was strolling the grounds of my family's estate when I felt three intruders scramble over the stone wall and land in the bushes. I guess they thought they were being quiet, but I can feel them through the earth, loud and clear. This'll surprise them.

WHOOSH! I made a mound of earth pop up beneath them, flinging them into the nearby bushes.

Surprise, surprise, the intruders are none

other than the Fancy Dancer and two of his friends! What does he want?

"What are you doing here, Twinkle Toes?"

"Well, a crazy king told me I had to find an Earthbender who listens to the earth. And then I had a vision in a magic swamp, and—"

What is this kid rambling on about?

The girl he was with interrupted him. "What Aang is trying to say is, he's the Avatar, and if he doesn't master Earthbending soon, he won't be able to defeat the Fire Lord."

The Avatar, huh? Well, that explains a lot! No wonder he was able to float through the air to evade me, and to redirect the boulder I shot at him. He can AIRBEND. So that's why Twinkle Toes is so light on his feet! Still, that has nothing to do with me.

"Not my problem. Now get out of here before I call the guards."

When they refused to leave I went into my helpless little girl act. I hate doing it, but some—times it serves its purpose. There's no way I'm going to let this guy ruin the cover I've got going. I cried out for the guards, who came running as they scrambled back over the wall.

"I thought I heard something," I told the guards. "I was scared."

"You know your father doesn't want you wandering the grounds without supervision!"

You know, it's funny that they think I'M the blind one. They're the ones who should open their eyes to the truth. Maybe someday I'll be able to be who I really am and not have to hide my ability. But not today.

Back at the house, my father pressed Master Yu about my Earthbending lessons. He wanted to make sure that I wasn't doing anything too dangerous.

"Absolutely not!" Master Yu said. "I'm keeping her at the beginner's level."

Ha! If he only knew! Of course, I had to sit there and listen to his nonsense, as usual. What kind of an Earthbending instructor can't spot potential and talent like mine? Like I said, I think they're the blind ones. I am so ready to break out of this . . . this prison.

Then one of the servants told my father that he had an unannounced visitor—the Avatar.

That kid just does not give up! Now he's wormed his way into my house using his title, which of course totally impresses my father. Well, I don't care what the Avatar does or says. I'm not going to become his Earthbending teacher. Besides, my father will never allow it.

So the Avatar and his two friends are joining me, my parents, and Master Yu for dinner. My parents are making such a fuss over the Avatar! I can tell this isn't going to be pretty. . . .

"Avatar Aang, it's an honor to have you visit us. You're welcome in our home as long as you like."

I think I'm going to be sick!

"In your opinion, how much longer do you think the war will last?" my father asked the Avatar.

"I'd like to defeat the Fire Lord by the end of summer, but I can't do that without finding an Earthbending teacher first."

I can feel him staring right at me!

"Master Yu is the finest teacher in the land," my father said. "He's been teaching Toph since she was little."

"Then she must be a great Earthbender!" the Avatar blurted out. "Good enough to teach someone else!"

What is he doing? This kid is going to get me into big trouble. He's going to blow every—thing. I can't let him tell my folks about my life as the Blind Bandit!

I slid my foot against the stone floor and sent an Earthbending jolt to the Avatar's leg. Hopefully that'll quiet him down.

"Sadly, because of her blindness, I don't think Toph will ever become a true master," my father said.

Just leave it at that, kid, all right!?

"Oh, I'm sure she's better than you think!"

Unbelievable! I expected the Avatar would be a little quicker on the uptake. Here, take another kick; maybe you'll get the message this time.

"What is your problem!" I shouted.

"What is YOUR problem?" the Avatar yelled, unleashing an Airbending blast that splattered soup all over everyone.

I wish he would just leave me ALONE!

I've spent most of tonight tossing and turning in my bed. Am I being too harsh? Am I taking out my own frustrating life on this kid who's just looking for some help? I should go talk to him.

When I walked into the Avatar's room, he jumped back and struck a defensive pose. I explained that I wasn't here to fight him and that I just wanted to talk. Isn't that what he said to me the first time we met? How ironic!

We took a walk through the estate's moonlit gardens, and I explained to him how I actually see through Earthbending. "But my parents don't understand. They've always treated me like I was helpless." He's kind of easy to talk to.

"Why stay here if you're not happy?"

He doesn't understand. They're my parents. "Where else am I supposed to go?"

"You could come with us."

He's got it pretty good, I suppose. He gets to go wherever he wants, without anyone telling him what to do. "You have a good life. It's just not MY life."

Just as I started to feel really sorry for myself, I felt movement nearby. People. Lots of them. All around us. "We're being ambushed. We've got to get out of here." I grabbed the Avatar's hand and hurried away, but a wall of earth rose up around us.

Earthbenders! Xin Fu and the others from Earth Rumble Six—I recognize their voices. How did they find me?

Before I could move, two metal cages dropped from above, trapping us inside.

I can't bend metal! Now there's no escape. Oh, no . . . they're hauling us away. . . . I think they are trying to get ransom money out of my parents!

They brought us back to the Earthbending arena where a short while later my father and Master Yu showed up, along with the Avatar's two friends. The Avatar's friend named Sokka gave back the money the Avatar had won, and Xin Fu released me.

But I can feel that the Avatar is still locked in his cage. It seems that Xin Fu plans to turn him over to the Fire Nation. He and the other Earthbenders are starting to carry off Aang's cage.

I feel sorry for Aang, but what am I supposed to do? My father is right here. I can't
give myself away; my life will be over. It's time
for me to go. . . .

"Toph, there are too many of them," Katara,
Aang's other friend (and Sokka's sister),
called out to me. "We need an Earthbender.
We need YOU."

"My daughter is blind, tiny, helpless, and
fragile."

Even though I've pretended to be those
things for so long, I'm not actually ANY of them,
and hearing my father say that makes me so
mad! You know what? I'm sick of pretending.
Why should I have to hide who I am because
my father can't accept me? If he loves me, he
should love me no matter what. . . . Enough is
enough. I can't let them take the Avatar away.
Katara is right. If I don't help him, the Avatar
will be handed over to the Fire Nation, and I
can't let that happen.

"My daughter cannot help you," my father
insisted.

"Yes, I can!" I let go of my father's hand and
headed back into the arena.

"Let him go!" I shouted at the Earthbenders. "I beat you all before and I'll do it again!"

⊕ ⊕ ⊕

Fighting in front of my father felt amazing! The Earthbenders tossed Aang's cage aside and charged at me. One by one I slammed them with my Earthbending, blocking their attacks and hurling them out of the ring. For that one moment I wished wasn't blind—just so I could see the expressions on my father's and Master Yu's faces.

Then I battled against Xin Fu. It didn't take me long to beat him as well. Meanwhile Aang tricked one of the Earthbenders into smashing his cage, which freed him.

"Your daughter is the greatest Earthbender I've ever seen!" Master Yu said to my father.

I can only imagine what my father must look like.

⊕ ⊕ ⊕

Now that we've all calmed down a bit from what happened earlier, it's time to talk to my father and finally tell him the truth. Here it goes. . . .

"It's true. I've been sneaking out at night to

fight in Earthbending tournaments. I'm sorry I didn't tell you, but I didn't think you would understand. You've always treated me like I was helpless, but I'm not."

Maybe he'll understand? Maybe I'm not giving him enough credit and he'll finally give me the freedom I've always craved, now that he knows what I can do. . . . And maybe I'll finally get the chance to make friends, something I've never had because I've always been so sheltered (more like locked up).

"I've let you have far too much freedom, Toph. From now on you will be cared for and guarded twenty-four hours a day!"

Then again, maybe he won't. This is unbelievable! Too much freedom? Yeah right! I'm not allowed to do anything or go anywhere, how is that freedom? And now I can't even roam my prison by myself. . . . This can't get any worse. My life is over. I'm stuck here, truly a prisoner in my own home. Stuck being the powerless little girl I created.

And now he's telling Aang and the others to leave. He says they are no longer welcome in our house. Great. And I have to stand here and watch my first and only friend walk out the door and out of my life. . . .

☷ ☷ ☷

I can't sleep—and the servant stationed at the edge of my bed isn't helping matters any. My mind is racing, but all I can think of is spending the rest of my life stuck here in this room in this house, burying who I really am deeper and deeper until she disappears completely.

Then Aang's words came drifting back to me. "You could come with us."

Aang is right. I DO crave the freedom that he and the others have. I DO want to experience the world, travel, and mostly stop pretending that I'm someone I'm not. I'm special. I can do things no one else can do. And if my father refuses to see that, then that's his problem. I'm twelve years old—old enough to know what I want—and I want to go with Aang. I want to teach him Earthbending. I want to have friends.

But how do I get away from this watchdog at the end of my bed, who follows my every move? Well, let's try this and see what happens. . . .

"I'm just going to the bathroom. I'm a big

girl. You don't have to come with me." That was easy! I tiptoed out of the room and locked the bathroom door. Silently, I slipped out the bathroom window. When I reached the ground I dashed through the gardens and leaped over the wall to freedom.

I only hope I'm not too late! I hope they haven't left yet! YES! There they are, at the top of the hill. But wait, I can't tell them the truth. I can't let them know that I disobeyed my father and ran away. I don't want them to tell me what I did was wrong, and I don't want Aang to feel responsible for my decision. This is my choice. Mine alone.

"My dad changed his mind," I lied. "He said I'm free to travel."

"You're going to be a great teacher, Toph," Aang said.

Wow, they're really excited that I can come. No one's ever really seemed to want me around or to miss me when I'm gone. It's kind of a nice feeling.

So, here I am, flying on the back of Aang's bison, with the whole world stretched out before me. Freedom! At long last, freedom!

Chapter 2

After flying for many hours we finally landed to set up camp for the night. I slid down off of Appa's back, and my feet touched nice, soft grass. At least it felt like grass. Turns out it was fur—bison fur. It's spring and Appa has started shedding something fierce.

I gathered up some fruit, nuts, and berries, so I'm all set as far as food goes. I'm just settling down against a rock and stretching out, drinking in my first full day of freedom— Ah, this is the life! Oh, here comes Katara. Wonder what she wants?

"So, Toph, usually when setting up camp,

we try to divide up the work between us."

"Hey, don't worry about me. I'm good."

Apparently she doesn't get it. She's going on and on about fetching water, building a fire, putting up the tents—all this stuff that has nothing to do with me. I can take care of myself. I always have. I don't need to be treated like a little kid. This is why I left home!

I get it—Katara is all rah-rah, go team. But the whole team thing just isn't my style. I've always been a loner, and just because I'm traveling with these guys doesn't mean I'm part of some group or something. I do stuff for ME. I carry my weight, without asking for anybody's assistance, like some dependant child. And they should do the same!

"I don't need a fire, I already collected my own food, and look . . ."

A quick Earthbending move should take care of a tent for me. A nice tent with rock walls. There! All done. "My tent's all set up!" But still Katara still doesn't look satisfied.

"Well, that's great for YOU. But we still need to finish—"

She really is annoying. What does she

want from me? I'm risking everything to come with them to help Aang learn Earthbending, and she won't stop hounding me about tents and water and firewood? I didn't leave home after being bossed around my whole life by my parents to be bossed around by her! "I don't understand what the problem is here!"

"Never mind . . ."

⊕ ⊕ ⊕

Later she came and apologized, saying that she was tired. Maybe that's why she's so cranky. I guess I should try to give her the benefit of the doubt. I accepted her apology and slipped into my rock tent to settle down for the night.

I had just fallen asleep when powerful vibrations rumbling through the earth woke me up. What is that? If I put my palms flat onto the ground, I'll be able to feel it.

This is something big. Very big. Whatever it is, it's powerful and it's heading our way.

I woke the others and suggested getting out of here. We scrambled onto Appa and took to the sky. Looking down they spotted a huge tank with thick treads and big missiles racing toward the spot where we had set up camp. We've got to get away from it, whatever it is.

We landed a good distance away. I stood for a moment and focused but felt no rumbling at all from that thing. We decided to settle there for the night, and that's when Katara started in again, asking me to help unload everybody else's stuff. I told her that I didn't ask her help unloading my stuff. How many times do I have to tell her that I carry my own weight!

"Ever since you joined us you've been selfish and unhelpful!" Katara screamed suddenly.

Selfish! I can't believe she said that. Selfish? I leave my cushy life to come here to help them and she thinks I'M selfish? I don't know what kind of fairy-tale world she's living in. "Listen, Sugar Queen. I gave up everything I had so I could teach Earthbending to Aang. So don't talk to me about selfish!"

I am done talking to the little princess. All I need is an earth tent—There! Now I'm shutting you out. In your face, sweetheart! I'm getting some sleep. Whoa—it's that thing again! I can feel it barreling toward us! Time to move, again!

For our third resting place we flew up to the top of a mountain. We all thought we'd be safe here, that the tank thing couldn't possibly find us much less follow us here. But we were wrong. I felt the vibrations shortly after we stopped. Then the others caught sight of black smoke rising over a hill, and now that thing is actually climbing up the mountain!

How does it keep finding us? Who's driving it? And what do they want with us? Katara and Sokka said they think it might be this guy named Zuko, the Fire Nation prince, who's been following them all over the world. Aang thinks we should stay and face whoever it is.

The tank just opened up! Three girls riding on mongoose-dragons are galloping toward us. Katara said she recognizes them as three girls they had fought in Omashu, before they picked me up.

Maybe Aang's right. Maybe we should just stand our ground. Between my bending, Aang's bending, and Katara's bending we should be able to take them. And if that doesn't work, Katara could always nag them to death.

Well, we're off on Appa, again. I had raised a wall of rock to block the girls, but one of them Firebended right through it! So we decided to leave again. But, as Aang pointed out, we can't keep flying forever. I, for one, am so tired I can't even think straight. And neither can Appa, apparently, because he just started to fall asleep in midair! I hate flying. Now we really have to land!

"Okay," Sokka said as we landed. "We've put a lot of distance between us and them. The plan right now is to follow Appa's lead and get some sleep!"

"Of course, we could've gotten some sleep earlier if Toph didn't have such issues with helping," Katara blurted out.

I can't believe she's still going on about that. I never asked any of them for anything. I've carried my weight from the start. Is she just trying to make me the scapegoat? That is so unfair. Besides, if this is anyone's fault, it's that big flying fur ball!

"If there's anyone to blame, it's Sheddy over there!" I just can't help myself anymore. If they want to play rough, I'll play rough!

"You're blaming Appa!"

Okay, Aang's mad.

"He's leaving a trail of fur everywhere he goes! That's how those girls have been follow-ing us."

"How dare you blame Appa! He saved your life three times today. If there's anyone to blame, it's you. You're always talking about how you carry your own weight. But you're not carrying your weight. Appa is. And he never had a problem flying when it was just the three of us and Momo!" (Momo is their pet lemur.)

I really hate it when people yell at me. If I wanted to be bossed around and yelled at, I could have just stayed home. Besides, what I'm saying is true! I might be blind, but I'm obviously the only one who can see that's how these girls have been following us. This is why I risked my relationship with my parents? This is who I'm traveling around like a nomad for? This is the kid who tracked me down and snuck into my house and hounded me to be his teacher? And now suddenly I'm nothing but deadweight to him and a punching bag to his friends? I don't need this. I don't need any of this!

"I'm out of here." I don't know where I'm going, but anyplace has got to be better than this.

⊕ ⊕ ⊕

I can't stop thinking about what happened earlier. All my life I've wanted to leave home, to be free, to travel and experience things and do whatever I wanted. This trip is supposed to be my chance. I've even gotten used to the idea of teaching the Avatar—it would have been kind of cool. But I never expected to be treated that way.

Katara wants me to behave the way she thinks is right. I had enough of that at home. And Aang—I never thought he would turn on me like that. I can't believe I was actually starting to trust him. I won't make that mistake again. With anyone. Besides, I—

Wait a minute—there's someone over there, I can feel him moving. A quick Earthbending shove should surprise him.

WHOOSH! I slammed my heel into the ground, sending a ripple that passed under the rock and struck the man hiding there—a heavyset man from the way he hit the ground.

I'm back on the rock, ready for my next attack, but he's just lying there, moaning.

"Ouch, that really hurt my tailbone."

Turns out he's just an old man. Nothing to worry about.

Then he did the weirdest thing: he invited me to his campsite for a cup of tea. Sure, why not. I've got nothing else to do, nowhere I HAVE to be.

"You seem a little too young to be traveling alone," he said when we reached his campsite.

"You seem a little too old."

He laughed. Then he poured a cup of tea and handed it to me. He wouldn't even let me pour my own tea. He's just like everyone else. "People see me and think I'm weak. They want to take care of me. But I can take care of myself."

"You sound like my nephew! Always think- ing you need to do things on your own, without anyone's support. There's nothing wrong with letting people who love you help you. Not that I love you—I just met you."

He may be a little cuckoo, but maybe he knows what he's talking about. It's just so hard to trust people. How do I know someone I trust won't turn on me, like Aang did? How do I protect myself from getting hurt? I guess I can't; not fully anyway. But maybe that's okay. Maybe that's just the chance I have to take if I'm going to have friends. Hmm, this old guy might be on to something. . . .

"So . . . where's your nephew?"

"His life has recently changed, and he's going through very difficult times, so he went away and I'm tracking him. He doesn't want me around right now, but if he needs me, I'll be there."

It's kind of amazing how much this old guy cares about his nephew. I mean, even though he ran away, this guy still understands that his nephew needs to figure it out on his own. I wish my parents understood that. . . . Anyway, I guess in order to care that much about some—one, you HAVE to trust them; and in order to do that, you have to actually let them inside. So you might get hurt, big deal! I can handle that. . . . After all, I am the Blind Bandit!

"Your nephew is very lucky, even if he doesn't know it." Okay, Toph, time to get out of here and go find Aang. "Thank you."

"My pleasure! Sharing tea with a fascinating stranger is one of life's true delights."

"No . . . thank you for what you said. It helped me."

Come to think of it, I was pretty harsh to Aang. He was only looking out for Appa, and it did sound like I was attacking Appa when I said the thing about him shedding. And I was kind of hard on Katara too. She's right; I have to learn to be part of the team now. Needing them isn't so bad. It's not like I LOVE being on my own. I've just been alone my whole life, because no one ever knew the real me. But Aang, Sokka, and Katara like me for who I really am, and for the first time in my life I can have friends. For the first time, I don't have to be alone. I've got to find them. Whatever happens next, I'm better off with them than without them.

"Maybe you should tell your nephew that you need him, too."

I left the old man, and now I'm heading back toward where I left everyone—but wait—I'm picking up the vibrations of a tremendous battle being fought. This fight is major! Powerful bending energy is being released, even buildings are crumbling! I have to follow these vibrations. . . .

What is this place? An abandoned city? There's Aang, Katara, and Sokka. They're battling that powerful Firebender who was following us in the tank. And there's that guy Zuko that Aang was telling me about, and— the old guy I just met? Something strange is going on here. . . .

Okay. Turns out the Firebender is Princess Azula of the Fire Nation. And to my surprise, the old man I met in the woods is actu- ally Zuko and Azula's uncle Iroh; he's fighting Azula. I can't believe that cool, old guy is from the Fire Nation, and I can't believe he's related to the Fire Lord. . . . But I can't think about that now. . . . Now it's time to get in on the action and blast Princess Azula's tights off.

WHOOSH! I cut loose an Earthbending blast, knocking Azula off her feet. "I thought you guys could use a little help," I called out to Aang and the others.

"Thanks," said Katara. Even SHE'S glad to see me. Time to corner the princess and see how tough she is, then. . . .

She seems to be accepting her defeat. . . . But wait! Oh, no! She just blasted my new friend, her uncle, down to the ground. I hope he's all right! He was so kind to me. Azula's going to pay for this!

We all simultaneously unleashed powerful bending blasts at her, but it's too late. She's gone, and Zuko's tending to his uncle.

"Zuko, I can help," Katara offered.

"Leave!" he shouted back, unleashing a fire blast just above our heads.

So we're back on Appa, flying away. I'm glad to be back with my friends. It feels like the right place to be, the place where I belong now. I'm ready to start teaching Earthbending to Aang. But right now, I'm just happy to finally get some sleep.

Chapter 3

We're camped in a rock quarry, which is turning out to be the perfect location to begin Aang's training. After a good night's sleep last night, I woke up early this morning—but not as early as Aang—who was already wide awake and raring to go hours before me.

"So, what move are you going to teach me first?" he asked anxiously. "Rock-a-lanche? The Trembler? Ooh, maybe I could learn to make a whirlpool out of land?"

"Let's start with Move-a-Rock."

This kid has no clue how hard this is. Time to see what he makes of these two boulders.

"The key to Earthbending is your stance. You've got to be steady and strong. Rock is a stubborn element—if you're going to move it, you've got to be like a rock yourself."

A little demonstration: just a quick thrust of the arms and WHAM! Right into the wall!

"Okay, you ready to give it a try?"

"I'm ready," he said without hesitation.

Okay, his feet feel set, and he's mimicking my movement. That's good. Ready, set, and—WHAT!? Great, instead of the rock moving, Aang just flew backward across the quarry. He's not firm, not thinking like an Earthbender.

"Maybe if I came at it from another angle—"

"No! You've got to stop thinking like an Airbender. There's no clever trick, no different angle to approach the problem. You've got to face it head on! Be rocklike. I see we've got a lot of work to do, Twinkle Toes!"

This is not good. He's still fancy dancing, tiptoeing his way around the rock. He'll never move it that way. Being light on his feet may be great for Airbending, but it's never going to help him become an Earthbender. Feels like

Katara is coming over to tell me something. I wonder what she wants. . . .

"Toph, I've been training Aang for a while now. He responds to a positive teaching experience—lots of encouragement and praise."

Here she goes, bossing me around again. And this time it's about something I know and she doesn't—Earthbending! I don't want to start arguing again, but how could treating him like a baby and encouraging his whining possibly help his Earthbending at all?

"Thanks, Katara. I'll try that."

Whatever, I'm just going to humor her. That is, until she's gone. Then I'm going to ride Aang hard until he learns what he needs to know.

For Aang's next series of exercises, I set up an obstacle course. I had him lift heavy boulders and move them through the course. Then I covered myself in rock armor and told him to try to stop me from pushing him. With Aang balanced on two rock pillars, I had him bend some smaller rocks from hand to hand. Then I suddenly slammed a section out of each of the pillars to see if he could balance . . . and he hasn't fallen, which means he's actually holding his stance! Finally he's taking a step forward.

Okay, now it's time for a more challenging test. Instead of moving a rock, I think I'll make him try to stop a rock. Yeah, stop it or be crushed by it. Simple but effective motivation.

"Okay, Aang, I'm going to roll that boulder down at you. If you have the attitude of an Earthbender, you'll stop the rock."

Just then Katara butt in again. "Sorry, Toph, but are you sure this is best way to teach Earthbending to Aang?"

Hmm, I have an idea. Sorry, Aang, but your good friend just made things a little harder for you. She's gonna love this. . . . "I'm glad you said something, Katara. Actually there is a better way." Better, not easier.

I put a blindfold on Aang. Now he'll have to feel the vibrations of the boulder to stop it. Welcome to my world! "Thank you, Katara."

"Yeah," Aang said, obviously unhappy with Little Miss Buttinski. "Thanks, Katara."

Okay, the boulder is on its journey down the hill, and Aang is getting into his horse stance. Good. His form feels perfect, his stance feels good. Now it's time to see whether or not he has the courage to stand his ground. Here we go. . . . That's good, just keep sticking your ground, be rocklike and sense the vibration. Come on Aang, you can do this. . . . It's getting closer, I can feel it, it's time to—What happened? Either it flattened him or he pulled a fancy-dancer move and jumped out of the way. . . . Well, he didn't get flattened because I can feel him coming toward me.

"I guess I just panicked . . . I don't know what to say."

"There's nothing TO say. You blew it. You had perfect stance and perfect form." What am I going to do with him? How can I teach him Earthbending if he's scared to Earthbend? How can the Avatar, who's supposed to save everyone, be such a wimp? "When it came right down to it you didn't have the guts. Do you have what it takes to face that rock like an Earthbender?"

"No. I don't think I do."

Great. Now I'm supposed to feel bad about hurting his feelings? HE messed up, and HE should feel bad about that. I'm not Katara, I'm not going to console him and let him cry on my shoulder. But here comes the Sugar Queen to make it all better.

No wonder he can't learn anything. He's so used to being treated like a little baby by Katara that he doesn't know what it's like to not always get everything right the first time around. The minute things get hard he gives up, and she rewards him for it. She thinks working on Waterbending is going to make him feel better. Well, it might do that, but it won't make him any better at Earthbending. I can't teach him if he doesn't have the courage to stand up to that rock.

Hmm. That gives me an idea. Maybe if I can get him to stand up to me, standing up to the rock won't seem so tough. Maybe if I get him mad enough . . . this ought to bug him.

"Hey, Aang, I found these nuts in your bag. I figured you wouldn't mind, and if you did, you're too much of a pushover to say anything."

He doesn't mind? He's happy to share? Blah, blah, blah, all this nicey—nice Avatar stuff is starting to get to me. Well, this next part will definitely bug him.

"I also have this great new nutcracker."

I dropped a nut onto the ground and smashed it open with his staff.

I felt him wince. He's getting testy now.

"Actually, Toph, I'd prefer if you didn't. That's an antique handcrafted by the monks."

Is this kid for real? Get angry, will you! I've just gone through your stuff without asking, and now I'm basically destroying your staff, and all you can say is "you'd rather I didn't"?

Here comes Katara again. What now?

"Aang, it's almost sundown and Sokka isn't back yet."

The two of them are heading off to find Sokka. I'll trail behind, just in case.

A short while later Aang found Sokka. Looks like he's wedged into a crack in the ground, playing with a little moose-lion cub. Where there's a cub, there's a mom . . . and there she is; I can feel her, not to mention smell her. Boy, she's huge, and she's NOT interested in playing. I could easily Earthbend Sokka out, but this will be a good test of Aang's courage. I'll just stay here, behind the tree, and listen. If things get out of hand, I'll step in.

No, no, no, no. Aang's using Airbending to push the lioness away. What is wrong with this kid? I thought he wanted to be an Earthbender. Doesn't he realize his fancy dancing isn't keeping her away? She'll do anything for her cub, and tiptoeing and floating around isn't going to stop her. Okay, wait a minute. I think he's getting ready to try some Earthbending. He's preparing an Earthbending stance; I can feel his feet firmly planted in the ground. Here we go. He's going to Earthbend . . . and . . . silence. What just happened? He didn't Earthbend, and yet I can feel the lioness moving backward, away from him. She's taking her cub . . . and she's leaving.

That's it, Aang! You stood your ground and it worked! That's what it's all about. This deserves a round of applause.

"You were here the whole time?" Aang asked when he heard me clap. "Why didn't you do something? Sokka was in trouble—I was in trouble!"

"Guess it just didn't occur to me." Okay, I'm just going to remind him that I still have his staff, and he should be good and angry . . . and ready for my final test.

I dropped a nut on the ground and lifted Aang's staff, preparing to slam it down.

"Enough. I want my staff back."

Perfect! He's furious with me. Exactly what I hoped for. "Do it now! Earthbend, Twinkle Toes! You just stood your ground against a crazed beast, and more impressive, you stood your ground against me. Do it!"

Okay, here we go, for real this time. He's setting himself up in a rock-solid Earthbending stance. Good positioning. Good form. Now, just thrust your arms forward, stay steady, and move that rock!

WHOOSH! Bingo! This time I definitely felt something move. "You did it, Aang! You're an Earthbender!"

And I'm a pretty good teacher—way better than Master Yu, anyhow.

"This is really touching, but can someone get me out of here?" Sokka blurted out.

"No problem," Aang said, preparing to Earthbend Sokka free.

"I'll do it, Aang. You're still new at this— you might accidentally crush him."

"Yeah, no crushing, please!"

Chapter 4

I've been working really hard with Aang every day for the past few weeks. He's improved his Earthbending and Waterbending significantly. We're all pretty tired from training and traveling, so we've decided to take short vacations.

At first Sokka objected, saying that we needed to find a map of the Fire Nation and come up with a plan to stop the Fire Lord once Aang was ready. But we promised him we'd spend his vacation tracking down the Fire Nation intelligence he was so keen on getting and he quieted down. He might be a total goof sometimes, but I do kind of admire his determination to kick some Fire Nation butt. Anyway, it was Katara's turn first, and she chose to go to the Misty Palms Oasis. Peace and quiet, here I come!

☸ ☸ ☸

We arrived at the place only to find that it was a rundown cantina—so much for lounging by the lake. But we did meet Professor Zei, head of anthropology at the university in Ba Sing Se, the Earth Kingdom's capitol. He told us he was searching for a library built by a great knowledge spirit named Wan Shi Tong. The library was hidden somewhere in the desert and was supposed to contain knowledge from all around the world.

Sokka got all excited because he decided that we're going to spend his vacation in the desert searching for the ancient library. He thinks that the library will have maps and other information about the Fire Nation.

If you ask me, that sounds like a horrible vacation. Who cares about some old library? I mean, I get that he's after the Fire Nation and all, but I really hate the desert. I just can't feel anything out there in the sand. I know there are some Earthbenders that live in the desert. They're actually called Sandbenders. In fact, there were quite a few hanging around the cantina when we arrived. But I can't Sand—bend, which basically means that in the desert I'm blind—really blind—without Earthbending to help me see. I'm not looking forward to this trip, but what can I do? I'm part of this team now, and there's no turning back. So, here we go, up onto Appa and off to the desert.

This is so boring! I can't even see, and I know there's absolutely nothing out there. Then the professor tells us that this place may not even exist! Great. This is most definitely not my idea of what a vacation should be. I've had enough of this. Time to have a little a fun.

"There it is!" Ha! Made them look. I can't believe they all listened to me! People, I'm blind, remember? "That's what it'll sound like when one of YOU spots it."

"Wait, down there," Sokka said anxiously. "What's that?"

Finally! Thank goodness! Time to land and get this over with already.

"Forget it," Katara cried suddenly. "It's obviously not what we're looking for. The building in this drawing is enormous."

"What kind of animal is that?" Sokka asked.

"That could be one of Wan Shi Tong's knowledge seekers, taking the form of a fox!" the professor said excitedly. "We must be close to the library!"

"No, this IS the library," Sokka said. "It's completely buried in the sand."

"Buried?" the professor cried as we landed. Then he fell to his knees. Is he going to start

weeping? He must think the library is ruined. Okay, Toph, time for a little reconnaissance, feel things out and see what the story is.

This stone spire is definitely part of a huge building, and it feels like that building is buried beneath the sand. But it feels whole.

"Guys, the inside seems to be completely intact . . . and it's huge!" This library must hold every book and map ever made.

◆ ◆ ◆

Apparently the knowledge seeker they were talking about climbed through a window on the side of the building. The others decided to follow it. Not me. Books don't do much for me. So I'm waiting outside with Appa.

Geez, Appa sure does scratch himself a lot. Talk about boring. When are they going to come back? I hope they find their maps and books and whatever else they wanted to get out of the library, or else this is a huge waste of time—Whoa, what's going on? I can't feel anything! Everything is shaking and the sand beneath my feet is disappearing. . . . Is the library sinking? If I could just get over there and feel it, I'd be able to tell—Oh no, it IS sinking. And everyone is still inside! This is awful. I've got to stop it. I have to keep the library from disappearing or the others are doomed. Who knows how far down it will sink?

This is why I hate sand—you can't get secure footing in grains that keep moving. I'm going to have to go ahead and do it anyway. Okay, fists tight, feet rooted . . . now push hard. Come on Toph, keep it from sinking! Fight the gravity, fight back!

What am I thinking? I can't hold this build-ing up forever. I'm not THAT strong. My feet keep slipping in this stupid sand. Come on, guys, get out of there—NOW! Please, hurry!

What's that rumbling? It sounds like it's coming from far away? Is something coming toward me? I can't deal with a new threat; I can barely handle this one! Well, whatever it is, it's moving very, very quickly. "Who's there?"

The sand, it feels like it's moving, and I'm not doing it. It's swirling around and around. That can only mean one thing: Sandbenders. What could they want?

Oh, no. They want Appa! How can I help him without letting go of the library and losing my friends inside?

I can hear the Sandbenders throwing ropes on Appa from every direction. They're trying to capture him. I can't just stand here! I have to let go and throw some earth their way, to slow them down. . . . WHOOSH! Take tha— Great. A sloppy cloud is all I can muster up? On solid ground I would have blasted them away. I'm useless here . . . and the library's sinking faster now than before!

What do I do? Let the library sink and try to stop the Sandbenders from taking Appa, or stop the building from slipping and lose Appa?

I can't win! I just can't. I'm sorry, Appa. I don't think I can help you in all this sand, but at least I have a small chance of saving Aang and the others. You understand that, don't you? Don't you? I'm sorry, buddy.

If the library would just stop sinking! I can't hold it! Where are you Aang?

Oh, wait, I can hear something. I hear people talking. They're out. Phew! I can finally let this thing go. Whoa, it's sinking all the way down, it's so far down I can't even feel it. . . .

Okay, now comes the hard part. Harder even than holding up that building. How do I tell Aang that I let those Sandbenders take Appa? That I couldn't stop them? I don't know how to tell him. I don't know what to say. I don't know how to make it better. I failed and I can't remember when I ever felt this bad.

"Where's Appa?" Aang asked.

I don't know, Aang, I don't know. . . . Be strong, Toph, and just tell him the truth.

"How could you let them take Appa?" Aang shouted. "Why didn't you stop them?"

"I couldn't stop them. The library was sink-ing. You guys were inside." Nothing he can say could make me feel any worse than I already do. And no explanation I give will be good enough. His best friend was taken. I'd be mad too.

"You could have come to get us! I could have saved him!"

"I can hardly feel vibrations out here. They snuck up on me. I couldn't do both—"

"You just didn't care! You never liked Appa! You wanted him gone!"

First the shedding comment and now this! No wonder he thinks I don't care about Appa. But that's not true, I promise! I never wanted this to happen. If we were on solid ground, I would have taken those guys apart. But I can't fight in the sand. I just can't. He's so mad at me . . . my first real friend, and this happens.

"Aang, stop it," Katara said. "You know Toph did all she could. She saved our lives!"

I guess I can't complain about Katara anymore; she's going to bat for me. Not that it matters, Aang isn't listening to her. Wow, he must really hate me if he won't even listen to Katara. And now he's flying off to try to find Appa. We're going to start trudging across the desert. I hope we spot Appa. . . .

Walking through the desert is so hard! I keep bumping into Sokka because I can't really feel where I'm going. And Katara has to keep turning me in the right direction so I don't wander off. Without a doubt, this is the low point of my entire life. Aang hates me, and I'm probably going to be stranded in the middle of the desert forever, and for the first time in my life, I actually FEEL like a blind girl. As we walked, Katara told me that in the library they discovered that there's going to be a solar eclipse soon and that if we get the Earth King to attack the Fire Nation on that day, the Fire Nation will be powerless without sun. If we get the Earth King to agree to the plan, we could actually defeat the Fire Nation. Imagine that?

After a long time Aang finally returned, having seen no sign of Appa. We all plopped down in the sand, depressed and hopeless. Then Katara started giving orders (she's good at that), telling us that if we didn't keep moving, we were going to die. I could have told her that. Then as we made our way over a dune, I stubbed my toe on something.

Man, did that hurt. And boy, do I hate not being able to feel where I'm going! What was that thing, anyway? It feels like . . . huh? "What idiot buried a boat in the desert?"

"It's one of the gliders the Sandbenders use," Katara said. "And look, it's got some kind of compass. Aang, you can bend a breeze so we can sail it!"

Maybe our luck is starting to change. Maybe we'll make it out of the desert after all.

We glided until we came to a giant rock cave. Katara hoped to find some water there. Aang hoped to find Sandbenders. Me? I'm just glad to get my feet back onto solid ground! Oh, this feels so good! I just have to stretch out and let my whole body come in contact with the rock.

But after a few seconds in the cave we started to hear strange sounds—of wings flapping and low buzzing. Suddenly we were surrounded by giant buzzard-wasps! They almost bit our heads off, but thankfully some Sandbenders came to our rescue. But even though they just saved us from the buzzard-wasps, I can tell that Aang's fury is growing.

Are these the Sandbenders who took Appa?

"What are you doing in our land with a sandsailer?" one of them asked. "From the looks of it, you stole it from the Hami tribe!"

"We're traveling with the Avatar," Katara explained. "Our bison was stolen, and we have to get to Ba Sing Se."

"You dare accuse our people of theft when you ride on a stolen sandsailer?" another Sandbender asked.

Wait a minute! I know that voice. That's the Sandbender who took Appa! I never forget a voice. I'm sure he's the one. No wonder he's overreacting. He's feeling guilty!

"Quiet, Ghashiun!" an older-sounding Sandbender shouted. "No one accused our people of anything."

"Sorry, Father."

"Aang," I whispered. "I recognize the son's voice. He's the one who stole Appa."

"Where is Appa? What did you do to him?" Aang suddenly yelled.

I've never seen Aang like this, not even when Appa was first taken—so enraged, so out of control. He just fired an Airbending blast that destroyed one of the sandsailers. I can feel the Sandbenders trembling nervously, but no one's saying or doing anything. And he just destroyed another one, even worse than he had the first. This is bad.

"Tell me where he is! Now!"

"It wasn't me!" Ghashiun cried.

"He's lying! I heard him tell the others to put a muzzle on Appa!" I'm not letting this kid get away with anything.

"I'm sorry!" Ghashiun finally cried. "I didn't know it belonged to the Avatar! I traded him to some nomads. He's probably in Ba Sing Se by now. They were going to sell him there."

Then the weirdest thing happened. Aang seemed to go into some kind of trance. I felt the wind whip up all around him, as if pure energy was radiating from his body. I was actually a bit scared, and I don't scare easily. But Katara was able to calm him down, and then he just collapsed in her arms, crying.

At least now we know where Appa is, except that it means we'll be going to Ba Sing Se, and I don't like that place.

Chapter 5

We're finally out of the desert and on our way to Ba Sing Se. Like I said, I don't like that city, but anything is better than the desert. Sokka studied a map he had taken from the spirit's library and discovered that there's only one way to get to there from where we are: by some thin strip of land called Serpent's Pass. Sounds creepy to me. . . .

On our way to Serpent's Pass we bumped into a family of refugees—a husband, his pregnant wife, and the wife's sister. They're also going to Ba Sing Se, and they told us about a ferry from a place called Full Moon

Bay that will take us there. They also told us Serpent's Pass is a deadly route.

Nice going, Sokka! Good choice.

We made it to Full Moon Bay, and we all got on line to buy tickets for the ferry.

The mean guard at the ticket counter won't sell Aang tickets because he, Sokka, and Katara don't have passports. I'm the only one with a passport, but I have a feeling that mine will be good enough for all of us. People just LOVE pleasing the Beifong family.

"I'll take care of this, Aang." Ha, I can't wait hear this guard's reaction. "My name is Toph Beifong and I'll need four tickets."

"Ah, the golden seal of the flying boar! It's my pleasure to help anyone of the Beifong family!"

See, it never fails! As much as I hated that stuffy mansion, there are times that being part of a wealthy, influential family has its advantages. This is one of those times.

While I was negotiating our entrance, Sokka ran into this girl Suki that he knows. She's one of the security officers, but she's also a Kyoshi warrior. And she OBVIOUSLY has a crush on him. Hmm. . . . I wonder if he feels the same way about her. He probably does. She feels all pretty and girly and light on her feet. Not that it really matters to me. I definitely don't care.

Just when I thought we were going to have a peaceful journey, the refugees told us their passports and tickets have just been stolen. Aang tried to talk to the ticket lady again, but she's not in the mood to listen. Now Aang's going to lead all of us through Serpent's Pass. So long quiet, peaceful boat ride. Hello, deadly pass.

Serpent's Pass is this thin ribbon of land with huge lakes on either side of it—these little adventures just keep getting worse. First, sand, which I can't bend; now, water, when I can't swim. . . . Oh, well, it's time to take the plunge. Our large group, including Suki and the refugee family, is starting to cross.

Sokka is being so annoying! He's all over Suki like that mother moose—lioness with her cub. "Are you sure you should be coming on this dangerous path, Suki?" "I wouldn't want anything to happen to you, Suki." "Don't sleep so close to that ledge, Suki. It may not be stable." Give me a break. I'm gonna barf. She's a warrior. I think she can take care of herself.

Whoa, a loud explosion just shook the path. I can feel an avalanche of rocks raining down from the side of the cliff above us!

"Fire Nation ships have spotted us!" Sokka shouted. He shoved Suki out of the way, but his move put him right in the path of the rocks.

Time to Earthbend a rock ledge above him. There, that'll protect him from the rocks. At least he's safe. And now he's dashing over to Suki, asking her if she's okay and telling her she needs to be more careful. Please! He's the one who should be careful—I just had to save HIS life! How about a little "thanks for saving my life, Toph." "Hey, no problem, Sokka, old buddy!" But no. He acts like I'm not even here. Whatever, I don't care. I don't need his thanks. Yuck—his fawning over Suki is so nauseating. How can she stand it? Okay, really, Toph, it's time to get over it. . . .

We just came to a spot where the path drops into the lake. Apparently there's a huge section of it that is completely covered with water. And I really can't swim! How am I going to get across?

"Everyone single file," Katara said.

Right! I'm traveling with a Waterbender.

Katara and Aang are lifting the water off the path, forming walls of water on either side of us. We're walking quickly through. I hate being so close to all this water, but I trust Katara. She'll get us across safely.

Just keep walking, Toph; soon you'll be away from all this water. What's that noise? I hear something snarling, and water's crashing down all around us. Time to switch it up with some Earthbending. . . . Here we go! Everyone up on my earth elevator. I'll just raise us above the splashing water; that should keep us safe from whatever it is. . . .

"It's a giant serpent!" Sokka cried. "I think I just figured out why they call it Serpent's Pass!"

Okay, well, I saved us from drowning, but now we're trapped on a tiny island of rock sticking out of the middle of the lake with a huge monster circling us! There's really no peace and quiet with this team, huh?

Katara just froze a strip of ice on the water's surface, connecting our little earth island to where the path resumes above the water level. It seems we're supposed to cross that while she and Aang jump into the water to battle the serpent with Waterbending and Airbending. I didn't think it could get worse than water and sand, but ice is worse than both. . . . This is awful! Wait, I can't feel anybody. Did everyone else cross already? So, I'm standing on this rock island, alone? I don't like this one bit.

"Toph, come on! It's just ice!"

Maybe it's just ice to you, Sokka, but to me it's a slippery surface I can't see or feel. Let me just put my toes on the ice and—No, no, I was right the first time. I'll just stay here on my little island. As long as that monster stays far away I—What's that crash? It's the serpent, and he's right behind me! Okay, that's it. No choice. Here I go. Here I go. I'm going. I'm—really—going! You did it! You're on the ice, just take little baby steps. Can't drift too far to the left or right or you'll end up in the lake.

"FOLLOW MY VOICE!" Sokka shouted.

As if it's that easy . . . okay, almost there,

almost—ahhhh! The serpent just smashed the ice bridge. "Help! I can't swim!"

"I'm coming, Toph!" I heard Sokka shout.

Surrounded by water . . . no sound, no sensation of touch. Total and complete isolation. Somebody better save me—quick! Oh, no! I'm sorry, Mom, Dad. I never meant to let you down. Maybe I shouldn't have left home. Maybe this whole freedom adventure thing was a big mistake. . . .

GASP. Strong arms . . . grabbing me . . . yanking me up! Ahhhh—air! I can breathe! Oh, Sokka! You saved me! Thank you, thank you. Sokka . . . my hero . . .

"Oh, Sokka, you saved me!"

I can't believe he dove in after me. This definitely deserves a kiss on the cheek, at least.

"Actually, it's me."

Oh, no. Is that Suki's voice? This can't be happening. I just made a complete fool of myself, didn't I? Getting all gushy over Sokka when the girl who really likes him is the one who saved me. Good move, Toph. Really slick.

"You can go ahead and let me drown now." Oh, why do I even care that he didn't rescue

me anyway? I'm safe, right? That's all that matters, isn't it? I'm back on dry land, and Aang
and Katara are safe too.

Our next stop is Ba Sing Se. Aang just
flew off to start looking for Appa. Suki's going
back to find her fellow Kyoshi warriors. But
first she's sharing a tender good-bye scene
with Sokka, complete with kissing. Yuck. It's
nauseating to listen to. . . . It's kind of nice to
be blind at moments like these. . . .

🀄 🀄 🀄

We made our way over to the base of Ba Sing
Se's outer wall. But we were shocked to find
Aang there.

"What are you doing here?" Katara asked.
"I thought you were looking for Appa."

"I was. But something stopped me. Something big."

Time for another earth elevator. Up we go!
Let's take a look for ourselves.

"It's a giant drill," Sokka said, "to cut through
the outer wall of the city."

So, the Fire Nation's built a drill to break
through the walls, and even the king's team
of elite Earthbenders don't seem to be able to

stop it. The city's in trouble. We need a plan.

"We'll take the drill down from the inside!" Sokka announced.

"By hitting its pressure points!" I added. Good idea, Sokka. You're actually not as big of a dud as you make yourself seem. . . .

"I'm going to give us some cover so we can sneak in," I told everyone. "Once I whip up some dust clouds, you're not going to be able to see, so stay close to me."

WHOOSH! "Run!"

Huh . . . this is one of the few times I can see and THEY can't. As long as I can still feel the ground with my feet, I'm golden. Okay, we're near the drill. Let me just open a hole in the ground and create a tunnel so we can get right up under it. Done.

"Everyone into the hole!"

"It's so dark down here," Sokka cried. "I can't see a thing!"

"Gee, Sokka, what a nightmare." Okay, I take it back. He IS a dud.

"There's an opening in the bottom of the drill," Sokka shouted. Aang's helping Katara and Sokka climb up into the drill.

No way I'm going in there! It's all metal. I can't bend metal, which means I'm blind in there. I'd be lost and useless. "I'll try to slow it down out here to give you more time."

Focus now. Concentrate, Toph, and . . . UP! If I can just jam this huge wedge of rock into the bottom of the drill to slow it down . . . Keep the energy coming. Keep it coming. It's too strong! It's pushing me backward. Come on, Toph, just dig your feet in, grab the ground. Ugh, my heels are digging up piles of earth behind me. I hope whatever they are doing in there, they're doing it fast!

It feels like I've been doing this for hours. The drill keeps creeping forward. I can't hold it anymore! I'm not doing any good here. I just wish there was something else I could—

Wait a minute! I hear voices down at the back end of the drill. Loud shrieking—I'd know those voices anywhere. It's Katara and Sokka arguing. But what are they doing back there? They're supposed to be inside the drill.

"You guys need some help?"

I found Sokka and Katara standing in what turned out to be a huge puddle of glop called slurry, a mixture of rock and water. Katara explained that it's been shooting through the drill and out an opening in the back end as it bore into the wall.

"Help me plug up this drain," Katara said. Together we bent the slurry back into the opening, to prevent it from pouring out.

So this stuff is SUPPOSED to come out. But, by trapping it inside, we are causing it to build up a lot of pressure. Whatever Aang is still doing in there, hopefully this will help him. We just have to keep pushing. Keep pushing. It's much easier working with Katara than try— ing to stop this monstrosity myself. Wait, I think it's time. It sounds like a tremendous crash is coming from the top of the drill.

"Here it comes!" This is so cool! The whole thing is lurching to the side, and slurry is exploding from every seam! Time to get out of the way. Up we go on another earth elevator . . . and there goes the slurry, gushing from the back of the drill.

I can hear the drill falling to pieces, and the motor is dead. It's finally over. We did it! We stopped the Fire Nation's drill!

Chapter 6

Now that that whole drill thing is over, we can finally start looking for Appa. So we're taking the train from the outer wall to the inner wall of Ba Sing Se. Everyone's excited to finally be in the city, but not me. Just when I was really enjoying the freedom of traveling, here we are back inside a city, trapped by a bunch of walls and rules. I have the same feeling I used to get back home. I know we have to find Appa and tell the king about the eclipse, but I'll be very happy when we finally get to leave this place.

We're finally at the station in the inner wall. I wonder how we're going to get around?

"Hello, my name is Joo Dee. I have the honor of showing the Avatar around Ba Sing Se. And you must be Sokka, Katara, and Toph."

Strange. This Joo Dee woman seems all nice and friendly, but she's so happy and bubbly and full of energy and good cheer. It's kind of creeping me out. How did she know that Aang was the Avatar? And how did she know the rest of our names, too? Who here knew we were coming?

"We have information about the Fire Nation that we need to deliver to the Earth King immediately," Sokka explained.

"Great!" Joo Dee replied in that sickeningly sweet voice. "Let's begin our tour."

She just completely blew Sokka off!

"Maybe you missed what I said. We need to talk to the king about the war. It's important."

"You're in Ba Sing Se now," she said. "Everyone is safe here."

How can she say that? We just saved them from a Fire Nation attack that could have brought down the entire city. I wish she knew how close she just came to becoming a prisoner of the Fire Nation. Safe is the last thing she is. There is definitely something weird about this woman!

I've seen this kind of behavior before—from my parents and my teachers. It's called "being handled." It's when adults don't listen to what you say. They just tell you what they want you to hear. We're not even in the city one full day and already I'm sick of this place. Boy, oh boy, it's going to be a long visit, I can feel it. . . .

And she's insisting on taking us on a tour of the city.

"What's inside that oval wall?" Katara asked.

"And who are those mean-looking guys in robes?" Sokka added.

"That is the royal palace," Joo Dee explained. "And those men are agents of the Dai Li. They are the guardians of all our traditions."

"Can we see the king now?" Aang blurted out.

Good for you, Aang. I'm tired of tiptoeing around this lady.

"Oh, no! One doesn't just pop in on the king. But your request to see the king is being processed, and should be put through in about a month! Much more quickly than usual!"

Is she for real? No way I'm staying in this place for a whole month!

☯ ☯ ☯

Joo Dee showed us to our house, but none of us were in the mood to relax. So we decided to walk through town searching for Appa. Joo Dee insisted on coming with us.

Unfortunately we've had no luck. No one has seen Appa, and no one even wants to talk to us. I don't think I'm going to survive here if everyone acts this way. It's so frustrating. It's like there's a big secret here that everyone's hiding and we're the only ones who don't know it!

☯ ☯ ☯

It's our second day in Ba Sing Se, and I'm hoping today is going to be better than yes—terday. Katara actually came up with a plan for us to see the king, so tonight Katara and I are getting all dressed up in fancy clothes and makeup, so we can sneak into a party the king is throwing. It's a perfect opportunity to tell him about our information!

At first the guards at the door wouldn't let us in, but then this guy Long Feng helped us get in. Then he wouldn't leave us alone until we found our "families." We were finally able to lose him. We were supposed to let Aang and Sokka in through the back door, but somehow Aang and Sokka snuck in without our help. Anyway, we're all inside now. Time to set the plan in motion.

"What are you doing here? You have to leave, or we'll all be in terrible trouble!"

That voice, it's so familiar. It's Joo Dee! We just can't get rid of her. But we can't let her stop us when we've gotten this far.

"Keep their attention while I find the Earth King," Sokka said to Aang.

Come on, Aang, just keep their attention until someone spots the king—Ahhhh! Who's grabbing me? Where are we going? This is not good. We're obviously not wanted here. I guess we're getting a little too close to whatever big secret makes this place so mysterious and makes everyone who lives here so frightened.

"Why won't you let us talk to the king?" Sokka shouted. "We have information that could defeat the Fire Nation!"

At least everyone is here with me. I wonder

who these guys are, and what they will do to us.

"The Earth King has no time to get involved with political squabbles and the day-to-day minutia of military activities," a man said.

It's that Long Feng guy. He's the cultural minister to the king and head of the Dai Li. What a liar! I bet he knew exactly who we were when he met us. And what kind of answer is that? What else could the king possibly be concerned with?

"But this could be the most important thing he's ever heard," Aang said.

"What's important to the king is maintain—ing the cultural heritage of Ba Sing Se," Long Feng shot back. "It's my job to oversee the rest of the city's resources, including the military."

"So the king is just a figurehead," Katara said.

Even though Long Feng's denying it, it's pretty obvious to me what's going on here. Long Feng has the power. He controls the city. And he keeps the king in the dark.

"You can't keep the truth from the people of the city!" Katara shouted. "They have to know."

"I'll tell them," Aang added. "I'll make sure everyone knows."

"I understand you've been looking for your bison," Long Feng retorted. "It would be a shame if you were not able to complete your quest."

Does this guy know where Appa is? I can feel Aang getting angrier by the second. And now I know that it's a really bad idea to make Aang mad.

Long Feng finally let us go. But as we were leaving, a woman came into the room and introduced herself as Joo Dee. But she's not the Joo Dee we know. She's someone completely different, claiming she's Joo Dee. Seriously, this city just keeps getting weirder and weirder. And I just keep liking it less and less.

Chapter 7

We've been putting posters up all around town, asking if anyone has seen Appa, but no one has. We've finally decided to take a break and return home. That's when Joo Dee—the original Joo Dee, not the second one— knocked on our door.

"What happened to you?" Sokka asked. "Did the Dai Li throw you into jail?"

"Of course not," she said. "I simply took a short vacation to Lake Laogai."

"Why are you here?" Aang asked.

"Putting up posters is not permitted. It's against the rules."

"We don't care about the rules!" Aang yelled. "We're finding Appa on our own, and you should just stay out of our way."

All right, Aang! I've been wanting to say that since I set foot in this place. Time to break some rules!

🔀 🔀 🔀

So we headed back out. While we were putting up posters, Katara ran into this kid named Jet that she knows from before. I don't know what he did to her in the past, but she's really mad at him.

"Katara, I swear I've changed," he pleaded. "I don't even have my gang now. I've put all that behind me. I'm here to help you find Appa."

"You're lying!"

Hmm, that's odd. I can feel his heartbeat and the vibrations his body's making as he breathes in and out. He's feels perfectly calm. His breathing is normal and his heart rate is steady. If he was lying, his heart rate would speed up and his breathing would grow faster and unsteady. No, this guy is telling the truth. "He's not lying."

🔀 🔀 🔀

Even though Katara is still skeptical, we've decided to follow Jet to this warehouse where he heard they were keeping Appa.

This place is empty! Appa's certainly not here. Maybe Katara is right about this guy. Maybe he's leading us into a trap. Maybe— Wait a minute. What's that? I'm stepping in something that feels very familiar. It feels like— oh. "Appa was here," I announced, reaching down, picking up a handful of his fur.

"We missed him," Aang said sadly.

"They took that big thing to Whale-tail Island—very, very far from here," said an unknown voice. Apparently the building janitor has seen Appa. Aang's insisting we go, no matter how far away it is. Jet said he'll help, but Katara still doesn't trust him.

Boy, oh boy, is she steamed up! Her heart is pounding like a hammer and her breathing is all over the place. Katara really likes this guy! "Was he your boyfriend or something?"

"No!"

Ha! She's totally lying. No wonder she's so mad at him.

As we got ready to leave, two people came

running over to Jet. They seem to know him.

"How did you get away from the Dai Li?" one of them asked him. Then she turned to Katara. "He got arrested by the Dai Li a couple of weeks ago."

"I don't know what she's talking about," Jet insisted.

Okay, now this is really weird. Impossible, in fact. The girl who's saying that Jet had been arrested, and Jet, who's insisting that he hadn't been, are BOTH telling the truth. Normal heart rates and breathing in both of them. How can that be?

"They both THINK they're telling the truth," Sokka discovered, "which means that Jet has been brainwashed!"

I guess he's not such a dud after all. That makes sense, finally.

"The Dai Li must have sent Jet to mislead us, and that janitor was part of their plot too," Katara said.

"I bet they have Appa right here in the city," Aang said excitedly. "Maybe they took him to the same place they took Jet. We need to find a way to jog his real memories."

So Katara's Waterbending a sparkling band of healing energy around Jet's head. Slowly he's beginning to relax. Soon his true memories are going to drift up through the brainwashing . . . and here it comes. Apparently, the Dai Li had taken him to their headquarters, underwater, beneath a lake.

"Joo Dee said she went on a vacation to Lake Laogai," Sokka recalled.

"That's it!" Jet cried. "Lake Laogai!"

Okay, now he's DEFINITELY telling the truth. I hope Appa's there, I really do. I can't wait to put this whole Appa mess behind me. If he's really gone, I don't know what I'll do.

We've finally arrived at Lake Laogai, but there's no sign of any kind of headquarters. There's nothing here. It's just a lake and—Whoa, wait a second! It's hollow beneath this rock! That's an entrance!

"Got it!" I shouted. I'll just Earthbend this rock up and—there it is, a tunnel leading under the lake. Okay, we're heading down now. It feels huge. . . .

"I think there might be a cell big enough to hold Appa up ahead," Jet said.

Again he's telling the truth. Please be in there, Appa. Please!

Okay, we're in and—

"Take them into custody!"

Long Feng! But Jet was telling the truth! He expected to find Appa here. Oh, well, it looks like instead of finding Appa we're going to be fighting Dai Li agents.

They're pretty good Earthbenders—very good, in fact. But nothing I can't handle, especially with help from the others. Is that all you got, Dai Li? You guys wouldn't even make it through Earth Rumble Six! You just—Oh, no! Aang said Long Feng's escaping!

Good, Aang and Jet are on it. Katara, Sokka, and I can finish up these Dai Li wimps.

🀄 🀄 🀄

By the time we caught up to Aang and Jet in the other room, Jet was lying on the ground. No sign of Long Feng, but things aren't looking so good for Jet. Katara's trying to heal him, but I can't tell if it's working. He's telling Katara that he'll be fine, but the sad thing is, this time, it feels like he's lying.

Back out into the tunnels. Focus, Toph, feel the spaces behind the doors. No, too small to hold Appa. Too small. Too—here it is! Behind that door. If he's in this tunnel he's in that room. In we go and—empty!

"He's gone!" Aang cried. "Long Feng beat us here."

"If we keep moving, maybe we can catch up with them!" Sokka said.

These tunnels are like mazes. Got to feel for the twists and turns and—the stairs! Here's the way back up! "Come on! Follow me!"

Finally, we made it—back out onto the shore. And we're surrounded by Dai Li troops—lots of them! Too many, from the feel of it. We can't take them all. I can't believe we came all this way and we didn't even find Appa. I can barely face Aang. I can only imagine what he must be feeling. This is all my fault.

Wait, what's Momo doing? He's chirping wildly like he knows something.

"Appa!" Aang shouted.

Appa's back! Yup, I'd know that unmistakable thud anywhere—even in the sand! I don't know how, but he's back. After Aang, I think I'm the most relieved person in the world.

☯ ☯ ☯

It didn't take Appa long to Airbend the Dai Li troops into the lake with his huge tail. Then he bit Long Feng on the leg and tossed him into the water too.

As uncomfortable as I am being off the ground and on Appa's back, I've never been so happy to climb up onto the big, smelly beast. Welcome back, Appa. Welcome back.

☯ ☯ ☯

Now that we have Appa there's nothing stopping us from telling the Earth King the truth about the war, the eclipse, and Long Feng's conspiracy for power. Well, almost nothing— except a bunch of royal Earthbending guards at the king's palace! We just have to keep battling our way in. . . .

Finally! We're face-to-face with the king in his throne room. Long Feng and some Dai Li agents are here too. Surprise, surprise.

"We need to talk to you!" Aang insisted.

"He's lying!" Long Feng shouted. "They're here to overthrow you."

"You invade my palace, lay waste to my guards, and you expect me to trust you?"

"He has a good point," I said.

But when he heard that Aang is the Avatar, the king decided to listen to us.

"There's a war going on right now—for the last hundred years, in fact," Aang explained. "The Dai Li's kept it secret from you. It's a conspiracy to control the city and to control you!"

After a lot of coaxing, the king agreed to allow us to prove our point. So we're taking him to Lake Laogai to show him the Dai Li's secret headquarters.

Okay, where's that entrance? Wait a minute. How can this be? Still, I can feel it with my feet. "It's gone! There's nothing down there anymore."

"The Dai Li must have destroyed the evidence," Katara said.

Great. Now the king will never believe us! Not that I blame him. I mean, our evidence doesn't exist anymore. But now Katara's pleading with him to come back and look at Ba Sing Se's outer wall. Hey, I know what she's going for here—great idea! She wants to show him the Fire Nation drill! There's still a chance. . . .

We're heading back toward the wall—there's the drill, right where we destroyed it! The king has to believe us now. . . .

"Dai Li, arrest Long Feng!" the king ordered.

Whoo hoo! He finally believes us. Now we're getting somewhere.

We were back in the throne room when a general named How arrived with some amazing news.

84

"We searched Long Feng's office," he said. "I think we've found something that will interest everybody. Secret files on everyone in Ba Sing Se, including you kids."

"It's a letter from your mom, Toph," Katara said. "She's here in the city, and she wants to see you!"

Wow! I can't believe my mom's here! I never thought she'd defy my father. . . . I thought my leaving would be the end of our relationship. But I guess Iroh's nephew, Zuko, isn't the only lucky one. . . . I guess my mother cares too.

I handed Katara the letter and asked her to read it to me.

It sounds like she's changed—a lot. Like she finally understands who I really am, and she's ready to accept me. This is almost too good to be true. For the first time in a long time, I really can't wait to see her!

Everybody else got good news too. Aang was given a scroll found on Appa's horn, telling him about a guru at the Eastern Air Temple who can help him with the Avatar state. And Katara and Sokka found out where their dad's Water Tribe fleet is.

It looks like we're all going our separate ways. Aang and Sokka are flying off on Appa—Sokka's going to find his dad, and Aang's off to find his guru. Katara is staying behind with the king. And I'm off to meet my mom.

I can't believe how sad I am that we're splitting up. These guys have definitely had an impact on me. I was wrong, thinking I could always do everything on my own. I need these guys. They're my friends. And I'm really, really going to miss them. But I can't pass up a chance to see my mom. Besides, we'll meet up again, I know it.

I'm off to this fancy apartment building where my mom's supposed to be waiting for me. Okay, here's the apartment, just breathe. It's going to be fine. She wants to see you, right? After all, she wrote that letter. She reached out and traveled all this distance. It's going to be better than fine. It's going to be great. Just stay calm.

KNOCK. KNOCK.

"Hello, Mom?"

KNOCK. KNOCK. That's odd. The door just swung open. "Anyone home?" Hmm . . . I guess I should go in.

"Hello!"

Something's very wrong here. This apartment is empty! There's no furniture. There's nothing here at all.

WHAM!

What's that? Something just dropped over me from above, surrounding me on all sides. Some kind of cage . . . a cage that I can't bend! It must be made of metal! "Who's here? And who do you think you're dealing with?"

"One loud—mouthed, little brat who's strayed too far from home."

I know that voice. It's Xin Fu from the Earth-bending arena!

How did he find me? He must have followed me all the way from home. So much for the loving, teary reunion with my mother. The letter, it was just a fake, a hoax, just to get me here. How could I be so stupid to think my mother would come all this way to tell me that she now understood me?

The cage is being lifted. I must be on some kind of platform. No, it's a carriage—with an ostrich—horse, by the sound and smell of it.

And now we're moving! I'm trapped. I wonder if the others are in trouble too? I don't know how, but I've got to get out of this cage! I've got to find my friends!

Chapter 8

88 We've been traveling for hours, I'm sure of it. But since I can't bend metal, I can't sense the vibrations of the ground or trees around me, and so I have no idea where we are. But from the sounds, the smell, and the bumpy ride, I think we're in a forest.

"I believe we need to go right."

THAT'S not Xin Fu, it's Master Yu! So he's in on this too.

"What are you talking about," Xin Fu replied. "The Beifong's estate is this way."

Hmm. Maybe I can use this to my advantage.

"Hey! Can you two old ladies quit bickering

for a second? I have to go to the bathroom!"

"Okay, but make it quick," Master Yu said.

"What's wrong with you?" Xin Fu shouted.

Great. NOW he's got brains!

"Very sneaky, Toph!" Master Yu said, trying to sound like he wasn't fooled. "Nice try, but you can't fool me."

"You may think you're the greatest Earthbender in the world, but even you can't bend metal!" Xin Fu added in his smug tone.

I need to get out of here! If only I COULD bend metal, I'd be out of here in a minute. Then those guys would be—

Wait a minute . . . metal comes from the earth. If I can bend it when it's still ore embedded deep in rocks, why shouldn't I be able to bend it in its processed form? It's the same stuff, right? Maybe it's not the METAL that's holding me prisoner, it's my mind. Sheesh. Now I'm starting to sound like Aang!

But what if it's true? Aang always had the power to Earthbend within him. It was only his approach that stopped him. Maybe that's my problem too. Okay. Here we go.

Hands against the back wall of the cage.

Focus, Toph. Focus. Go back to day one, the first time you ever moved a rock. Remember, that seemed so hard until you found the right place in your mind, the right level of concentration. After that, it was a snap.

Come on, metal, bend, bend! Nothing. Okay, deep breath, then try again.

Bend, metal. You can't hold me back. You can't box in willpower. I am rooted. I am solid. You will bend!

My hands are trembling. I can feel power surging from deep within me. The metal is starting to buckle. Yes! Toph, you rule! Okay, okay, don't get carried away. Take that feeling and build on it. Focus. Harder, harder. Push!

The back wall of the cage is ripping open. I'm free! I'm out of that cage! And I've gained a whole new Earthbending skill in the bargain.

I'll just slip around to the front of the carriage and give those clowns a surprise.

"What was that noise?" Master Yu asked.

"It must be one of her tricks," Xin Fu replied.

"It's no trick," I said, standing right beside them. "And neither is this."

WHOOSH! Take that, you clowns! Now it's your turn in the cage. I'll just Metalbend the cage shut—I love this! There, now you're trapped. How does it feel, boys? "I AM the greatest Earthbender in the world. And don't you two dunderheads ever forget it!"

⊕ ⊕ ⊕

Finally—free again! I'll just ride this Earthwave back toward Ba Sing Se. Freedom tastes especially sweet today, knowing that there is now one less element that can hold me!

Too bad about that letter, though. Too bad it wasn't real. It would be really great if my folks could understand and accept me. Yeah, like that's ever going to happen.

Wheeee! This is the only way to fly—with my feet still on the ground! Man, Earthwave riding is the best. Once I get there, I've got to see if Katara and the others are all right. I mean, if the letter from my mom is a fake, who knows about Katara's dad and Aang's guru. I—

Whoa! What's that! Something swooping down from the sky. I'm losing the wave! I'm crashing down—

BOOM! Appa? "Hey! Don't sneak up on me like that!"

'"Need a ride?"

Sokka's here too! I guess I'll be riding Appa the rest of the way—oh, joy.

⊕ ⊕ ⊕

On our way back Aang told me that while he was with the guru, he had a vision that Katara was in trouble. That's why he left. He picked up Sokka on the way. Gosh, I hope that Katara's okay. I hope Aang's vision isn't real. . . .

We're back at our house in Ba Sing Se, but

Katara isn't home.

"Katara IS in trouble," Aang said. "I knew it!"

And now I can feel someone else is coming. "Someone's at the door." I recognize the footfall. "Actually, I know who it is. It's an old friend of mine." I flung the door open, and sure enough, it's Iroh.

"I need your help."

"You know each other?" Aang asked.

"I met him in the woods once, and knocked him down. Then he gave me tea and some very good advice."

I invited him in. Sokka immediately took up a warrior's stance. "I'm warning you. If you make one false move . . ."

Give him a break, Sokka. This guy seems about as dangerous as a soggy tea leaf.

"Princess Azula is in Ba Sing Se," the old man began.

"She must have Katara!" Aang said.

"She has captured my nephew as well."

"Then we'll work together to fight Azula, and save Katara and Zuko," Aang said.

The old man brought along a Dai Li agent he had captured. Intimidated by a bunch of angry benders, the guy talked right away. "Azula and Long Feng are plotting a coup. They're going to overthrow the Earth King."

"Where are they keeping Katara?" Sokka insisted.

"In the crystal catacombs of Old Ba Sing Se, deep beneath the palace!"

I wasn't here to help Katara before. But I'm going to help her now. I'm going to find those catacombs.

We're hurrying to the palace courtyard. Hmm . . . I can't feel anything. Everything seems pretty solid. "If there's an ancient city down there, it's deep." I'll just blast them open. Yup, the catacombs are definitely down there.

"We should split up," Sokka suggested. "Aang, you go with Iroh to look for Katara and the angry jerk. No offense . . ."

"None taken," Iroh replied.

"And I'll go with Toph to warn the king about Azula's coup."

✦ ✦ ✦

94 Okay, we're close to the palace; the Dai Li is arresting General How!

"The coup is happening right now!" Sokka said. "We've got to warn the Earth King!"

We're in the throne room. Something feels strange to me. Huh? Who's that? Feels like a Kyoshi warrior. And she's heading right for Sokka. If Suki thinks we have time for smooches, she's sorely mistaken. . . .

"Hi, cutie," she cooed.

Wait a minute—that's not Suki! And that's a voice I've heard before. "They're not the real Kyoshi warriors!"

Oh, boy, I can feel darts heading right at me! I'll raise a stone slab. This is crazy. I mean, I like bending just as much as the next person, but when will this madness stop!

"This fight is over."

Azula! And it sounds like she's standing right next to the king. She's right. The fight is over. We can't risk endangering the king. One quick fire blast from her and the king would be seriously hurt. We have to give up. . . .

So, Azula's Dai Li agents led me, Sokka, Momo, and the Earth King out of the throne room, and have locked us in what they called an "Earthbender-proof" prison cell. In other words, it's made out of metal.

Beautiful! I love surprising the bad guys. This is one of those times I'm sad I'm blind . . . I have to miss out on seeing their shocked faces!

Here you go, Toph, you can do this again. Channel the energy . . . NOW!

The metal cell door is open. Time to make a dash for the entrance to the tunnel. Almost there, almost—Wait, someone's heading toward us. It's Katara! But where's Aang?

Oh, no! He's hurt! She's carrying him.

Just then Appa swept down and picked us up—me, Sokka, Katara, Momo, the Earth King, the king's pet bear, and Aang, stretched out motionless on Appa's soft fur.

Katara's using her healing water to revive him. His eyes are open! Oh, thank goodness!

But, you know, I wonder if any of us is really going to be okay. I mean, the Earth Kingdom has fallen to Azula and the Fire Nation. Now what do we do? We thought we were doing the right thing, we thought delivering that message would make everything all right. We thought it would end the war.

But now that hope is gone. Azula has control of the Earth Kingdom, and once again we're on the run. Don't get me wrong, I wouldn't want to be on the run with any other team. I'm glad I met Sokka, Katara, and Aang—even Appa and Momo.

But what happens next? I wish someone had the answer, because I have no idea. I guess I'll just do what I always do: feel my way through and hope for the best.